Dirty Bertie

TOOTHY!

For Ismail – another book for your collection
~ D R
For Laurie and Ed – the best kind of friends
~ A M

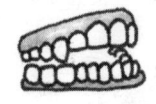

STRIPES PUBLISHING
An imprint of Little Tiger Press
I The Coda Centre, 189 Munster Road,
London SW6 6AW

A paperback original
First published in Great Britain in 2013

Characters created by David Roberts
Text copyright © Alan MacDonald, 2013
Illustrations copyright © David Roberts, 2013

ISBN: 978-1-84715-363-0

The right of Alan MacDonald and David Roberts to
be identified as the author and illustrator of this work
respectively has been asserted by them in accordance
with the Copyright, Designs and Patents Act, 1988.

Printed and bound in the UK.

10 9 8 7 6 5 4 3 2 I

Dirty Bertie

TOOTHY!

DAVID ROBERTS WRITTEN BY ALAN MACDONALD

Stripes

Collect all the Dirty Bertie books!

Contents

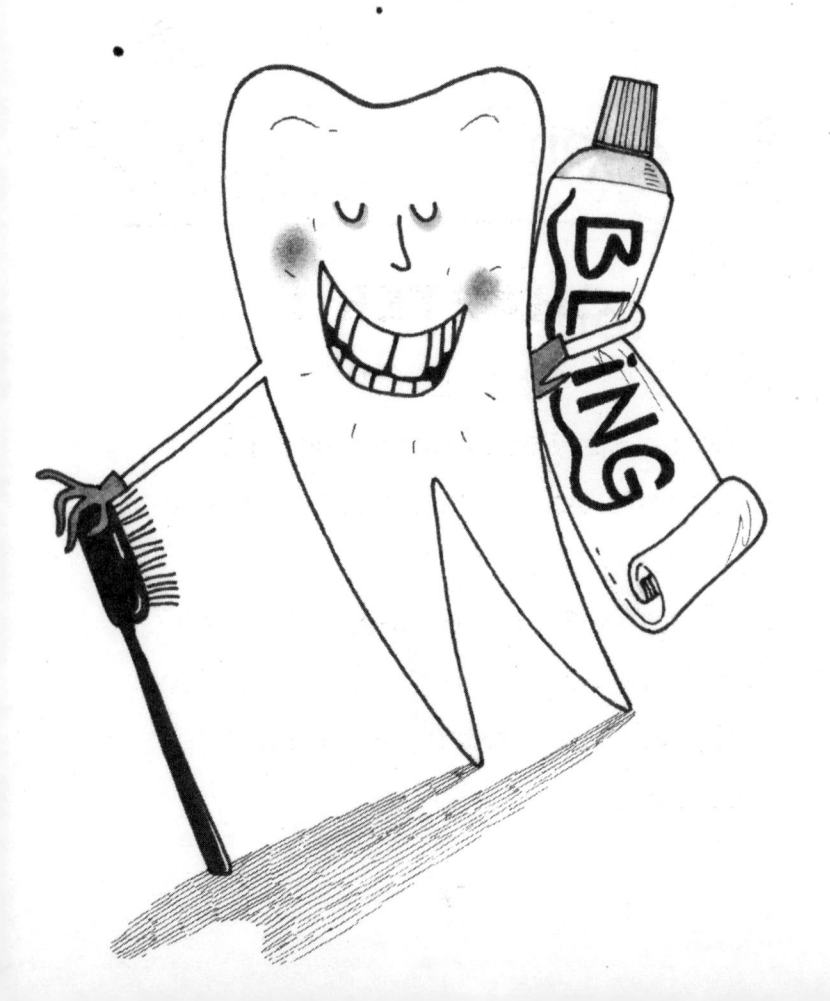

CHAPTER 1

MUNCH! CRUNCH!

Bertie was back from school and raiding the biscuit tin. Uh-oh! Mum was coming.

"Put it back, Bertie," she said. "Don't forget you've got the dentist tomorrow."

Bertie's legs suddenly felt weak. His eyes bulged.

Dirty Bertie

"The dentist?"

"Yes," said Mum. "You and Suzy are due for a check-up."

"But … but I went before!" stammered Bertie.

"That was last year," said Mum.

Suzy looked up from her homework.

"I *like* going to the dentist," she said. "Mr Filling says I've got perfect teeth."

Bertie stuck out his tongue at her.

Dirty Bertie

"Just 'cos you're scared," jeered Suzy.

"I'm not!" said Bertie.

"You are!" said Suzy. "Last time Mum had to drag you there."

That was a lie, thought Bertie. He'd hung on to the lamp post because he was worried they were early. Besides, it wasn't his fault that their dentist looked scary. Mr Filling had big hairy hands and mad eyes. He wore a mask over his mouth. Bertie thought he looked like a murderer.

In any case, there was nothing wrong with his teeth. None of them had fallen out, so why did he have to go? Wait a moment … didn't Mum say his check-up was tomorrow? He was saved!

"I can't go!" he said. "I've got school."

"Don't worry," said Mum. "I dropped a note in to Miss Boot this morning."

Dirty Bertie

Bertie groaned.

"Anyway," said Mum, "if you clean your teeth you've nothing to worry about."

"I clean MY teeth!" boasted Suzy.

Bertie frowned. He did clean his teeth — just not every day. It saved time just to slosh water round his mouth. Now and again he used toothpaste, but mainly for drawing faces on the mirror.

He ran his tongue over his teeth. Hmm, they did feel a bit furry. What if they were crawling with toothy germs? He might need to have something done — a filling or even a tooth out! Darren said that his dentist pulled teeth out with his bare hands.

Dirty Bertie

Bertie gulped. He needed to think of
an excuse quickly. Wait! Mum said she'd
written Miss Boot a note. So what was
to stop Miss Boot writing back? Bertie
rushed upstairs to find a pencil and
paper.

Deer Missus Burns,

Just to let you kno Bertie sore
the skool dentist today. he sed
Bertie's teeth was the best in
the class. They are so good he
do not need to see the dentist
agane. Not never.

Miss Boote (Teecher)

That should do it, thought Bertie, folding the letter in two.

He took it downstairs and waited as Mum read it through. She frowned.

"I see, and Miss Boot wrote this, did she?"

Bertie nodded. "This afternoon."

"Strange," said Mum. "Her handwriting is exactly like yours."

"Um … is it?" said Bertie.

"Yes," said Mum. "And she can't spell her own name."

She screwed up the letter and tossed it in the bin.

"Nice try, Bertie," she said. "But you are going to the dentist and that's final."

CHAPTER 2

"Ah, Bertie," breathed Mr Filling. "I've been waiting for you."

Bertie was pushed back into a chair. CLUNK! Iron rings snapped down over his wrists. He was a prisoner.

"Now, let's have a look, shall we?" cackled Mr Filling. The mask over his face slipped down, revealing two sharp fangs.

Dirty Bertie

"ARGHHHHH!"

Bertie woke up in bed clutching his pillow. He opened his eyes. Thank goodness, it was only a nightmare.

What day was it today? Just a normal school day – maths, English, then... Bertie turned cold. Then THE DENTIST. HELP!

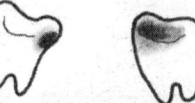

Later that day, Bertie sat in the dentist's waiting room. Suzy yawned. Mum was reading a magazine. None of the other people in the waiting room seemed nervous at all.

Bertie stared at a poster on the opposite wall. A large smiley tooth said *Brush your teeth!*

Bertie wished he was back in school – anything was better than this.

He slumped back in his chair with a groan.

"What's the matter? Scared?" said Suzy.

"Course not," said Bertie.

"You're such a baby," said Suzy.

"I'm not," scowled Bertie. "And I'm not afraid of the dentist either."

"Good," said Suzy. "Then you won't mind going first."

Bertie turned pale. Go first? Why couldn't he go last? Or better still go home?

He gripped his seat. From now on he vowed to clean his teeth ten times a day. He would even use toothpaste. He would give up sweets – apart from jelly snakes, obviously.

The dental nurse came in. "Bertie and Suzy Burns? Who's going first?" she asked.

"Bertie," said Suzy, pointing to him.

Bertie got shakily to his feet. This was it. He was a dead man.

"Good luck!" whispered Suzy. "Don't wet your pants."

"Do you want me to come with you?" asked Mum.

Bertie shook his head. He wasn't a baby.

The nurse had gone ahead. Bertie
dragged himself down the corridor. Mr
Filling's surgery was the last room on the
left. The door was slightly open and he
could hear the dentist's booming voice.

"Yes, it's a real shame," he said. "He's
only seven years old."

"Is there nothing you can do?" the
nurse asked.

"Afraid not. It's the kindest way, he'll have to be put to sleep."

Bertie froze. His blood ran cold. Had he imagined it? No, he'd heard it with his own ears. The dentist was planning to put him to sleep … in other words, bump him off! Bertie gulped. Hadn't he always said Mr Filling looked like a murderer? That explained why he wore gloves, so he didn't leave fingerprints!

Bertie looked around wildly. He could run back and tell his mum. But she'd never believe him. "Mr Filling — a murderer? Don't be silly, Bertie," she'd laugh. No, there was only one thing for it — he had to escape. Bertie spotted a cloakroom to his right. He slipped inside and closed the door.

CHAPTER 3

Bertie paced up and down, trying to stay calm. He had to get out of here before the mad murderer came for him. The nurse was obviously his evil assistant — she'd probably been hypnotized. Somehow he had to make it past the receptionist without getting caught. But how?

Dirty Bertie

He looked around. Maybe he could escape through the window? But it was too high up. Or down the toilet? But what if he got stuck? His eye fell on some hats and coats hanging up beside the door. A disguise!

A minute later, Bertie slipped out of the cloakroom. He was dressed in a big grey overcoat, which dragged on the floor. He had a trilby hat pulled down over his eyes and a scarf wound round his face. He swept down the hall, trying hard not to trip on his coat-tails.

"Mr Froggat?"

Bertie halted. Did the receptionist mean him? He looked around. There was no one else about.

"Mr Froggat, if you've got a moment, please?" said the receptionist.

Bertie shuffled over to the desk, keeping his head down. The hat was too big and kept slipping over his eyes.

"We just need to book your next appointment," said the receptionist. "When would you like to come?"

Bertie wobbled his head.

"Umm num num," he mumbled.

"Sorry?" said the receptionist.

Bertie flapped his long sleeves.

"Umm num num," he repeated.

"I see," nodded the receptionist, who hadn't understood a word.

"WHAT ABOUT THE 24th, MR FROGGAT?" she shouted, as if he was deaf. "IT'S A THURSDAY!"

Bertie nodded. He didn't care what day it was, as long as he could go. The receptionist scribbled the date on a card and handed it to him.

"IS THAT ALL RIGHT?" she yelled.

"Num. Umm num," mumbled Bertie, taking the card. He hurried away. It was touch and go, but he thought he'd got away with it. All he had to do now was make it down the stairs.

"Excuse me!"

A hand tapped him on the shoulder. Argh! It was his mum!

"Have you seen a small boy?" she asked. "About this big with a runny nose?"

Bertie shook his head firmly. The hat slipped over his eyes and fell off.

Uh-oh. There was only one thing to do. Run for it!

He made a dash for the stairs, but it was no use. Mum had hold of his scarf. She reeled him in.

"And where do you think you're off to?" she said.

CHAPTER 4

Mum dragged Bertie back down the corridor to the surgery. Mr Filling turned round.

"Ah, Bertie, found you at last!" he beamed. "Trying to escape, were you? Ha ha!"

Mr Filling had a round face with eyebrows that danced around like hairy caterpillars. Bertie stared at his big hands.

"Jump up and have a seat then," he said, patting the chair. For a murderer he seemed in a pretty good mood.

Bertie looked back at Mum, who folded her arms. There was no way out. He sat down in the black leather chair. It rose up, humming as it tilted backwards. He found himself staring at pictures of dancing elephants on the ceiling.

"Okay, young man? Comfortable?" boomed Mr Filling.

Bertie nodded. His hands were starting to sweat. What was the dentist's evil plan? A deadly injection? Poisonous mouthwash? Mr Filling's masked face loomed into view. Bertie stared at his mad eyes.

"Open wide…" he said, picking up a long silver instrument.

"YEEEEEAAAARGHH!"

Bertie leaped from the chair as if he'd been shot from a catapult. He grabbed a giant toothbrush from a display.

"Keep back or I'll use it!" he cried.

Mr Filling's hairy eyebrows shot skywards. Mum advanced. Bertie bolted out of the door.

Dirty Bertie

"Bertie! Get back here!" shouted Mum.
In the hallway, Bertie almost ran into
the receptionist. He swerved left and
burst into the waiting room. People
looked up from their magazines in
surprise.

Dirty Bertie

"Hide me!" Bertie panted, waving his toothbrush.

Suzy rolled her eyes. "What are you on about?"

"Quick, he's coming! He's going to murder me!"

Dirty Bertie

Footsteps came down the hallway. There was no time to argue. Bertie ducked behind the curtains and pulled them around him. He stood there, trying not to breathe.

Mr Filling, Mum and the dental nurse marched in.

"Where is he?" demanded Mum.

Suzy sighed. She pointed to the curtain where two dirty trainers were poking out.

Mum went over and yanked it back.

"Bertie, what are you playing at?" she cried.

"Don't let him get me!" begged Bertie.

"Who?"

"Mr Filling! He's a murderer!"

A gasp went up. Every head in the waiting room turned to look at the dentist.

Mr Filling laughed weakly. "What are you talking about? I just want to examine your teeth!"

"I heard you," said Bertie. "I heard you say you were going to put me to sleep."

Mr Filling looked baffled. Then it came back to him. "OH! I was talking about Rex," he laughed.

Dirty Bertie

"Rex?"

"Yes, my dog. He's very ill and the vet says it's kindest to put him to sleep."

The heads all turned back to Bertie.

"Oh, I see … your dog," he mumbled.

Mum marched over and grabbed him. "Now, can we *please* get this over with?" she said.

Dirty Bertie

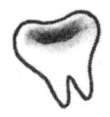 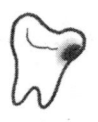 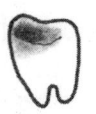

Bertie lay back in the dentist's chair while Mr Filling examined his teeth. *It wasn't my fault,* he thought. *Anyone can make a mistake.*

Mr Filling took off his mask.

"There, all done," he said.

Bertie blinked. That was it? No injections? No fillings? He hadn't felt a thing. He sat up, feeling a bit foolish. Suzy would never let him forget this. Wait till the story got round school – Bertie hiding from the dentist. He'd never hear the last of it. "Scaredy-cat! Cowardy custard!" they'd call after him.

"Your teeth are fine," said Mr Filling. "Just don't forget to clean them."

Bertie climbed down from the chair.

"I'm sorry about … you know … before," he mumbled.

Mr Filling laughed.

"Oh, don't worry, I'm used to nervous patients. Your sister used to be the worst."

"Suzy?" said Bertie. This was news to him.

"Oh, yes, she used to scream if I came near her," smiled Mr Filling. "I had to give her Mr Teddikins to cuddle." He pointed to a large, goggle-eyed teddy bear in the corner.

Bertie smiled to himself. Mr Teddikins, eh? Wait till the next time Suzy called him a cry baby. She was never going to tease him again!

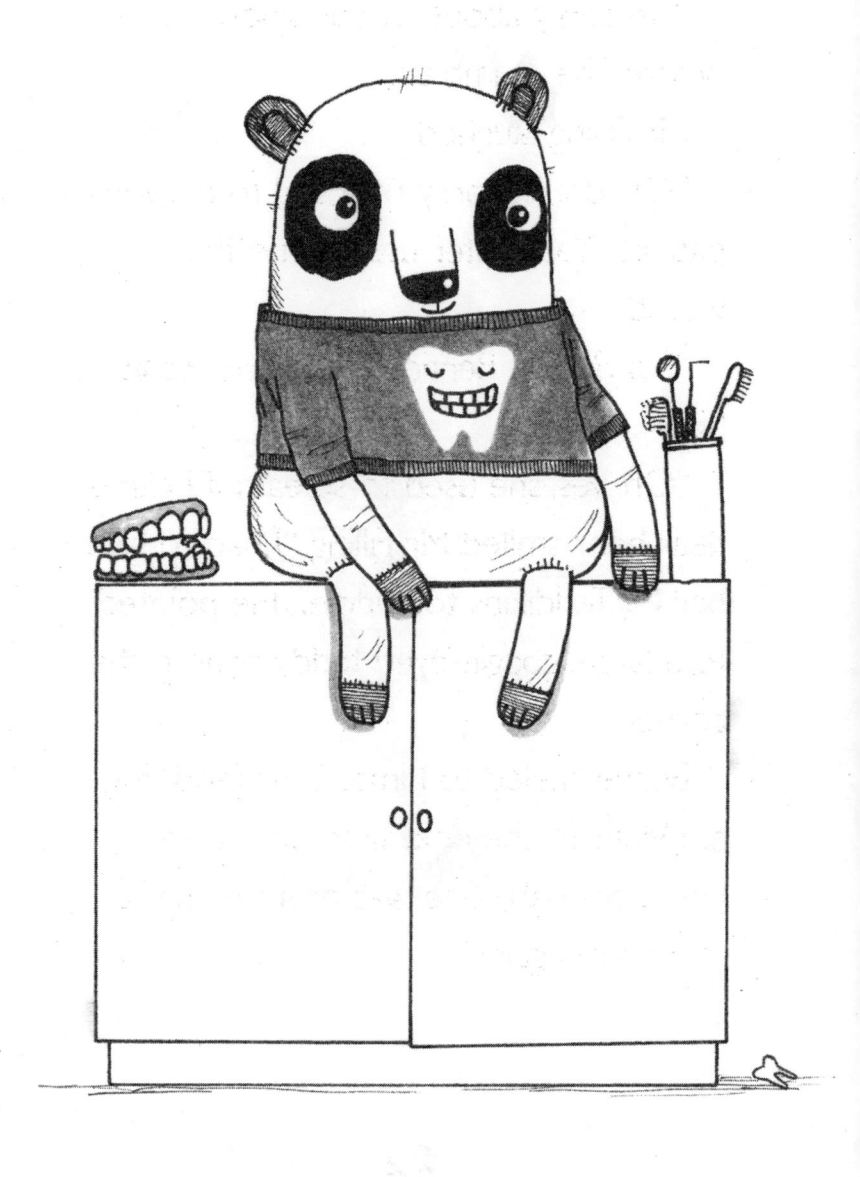

CHAPTER 1

Mum burst into the kitchen excitedly.

"The holiday's booked!" she said. "And we're flying out!"

Suzy whooped. Dad groaned. Bertie almost fainted. Had he heard right? Was he dreaming?

"Flying?" he said.

"That's right," said Mum.

Dirty Bertie

"On a plane?"

"Of course on a plane, how else?"

"WAHOO!"

Bertie had never flown in his life. Loads of his friends had been on planes. Eugene said it was amazing. They showed films and brought you free drinks! Royston Rich claimed he'd been up in his dad's private jet. But Bertie had never even been to an airport. Whenever they'd talked about flying, Dad always found an excuse.

Dirty Bertie

"Is Whiffer coming?" asked Bertie.

"Dogs aren't allowed on planes," said Dad. "Now, on the car ferry—"

"Don't start," sighed Mum wearily. "We agreed."

"Where are we sitting? Can I sit next to the pilot?" asked Bertie.

"No," said Dad firmly. "You sit where you're told."

Bertie didn't think Dad sounded that thrilled to be going on a plane. But *he* was. Wait till he told Darren and Eugene!

"When do we go?" asked Suzy.

"In half term. That's three weeks," said Mum.

THREE WHOLE WEEKS! That was ages! Bertie didn't think he could wait that long.

"EEEEOWWW!" he cried, taking off

and zooming round the kitchen. He
swooped down at supersonic speed,
then trod in Whiffer's bowl and
skidded…

"Yarghhh!"

CRASH!

"BERTIE!" yelled Dad.

Bertie scrambled to his feet. Honestly,
some people were so touchy!

CHAPTER 2

Three weeks later, the great day finally dawned. Bertie was so excited he'd been dressed since 5 a.m. His bag had been packed for weeks. He had everything he needed for the flight: sweets, comics, his Jumbo Jet Sticker Book and more sweets, in case he ran out.

At the airport, Dad loaded the cases

on to a trolley and they went inside.
Bertie hurried past the shops and cafés.

"Can we get on the plane now?" he
said. "I want to get a good seat."

Suzy rolled her eyes. "It's not going for
hours! We need tickets."

"Yes," said Mum. "First we have to
check in and get our boarding passes."

The queue at the desk tailed back for
about a mile. Bertie stared in horror.

"What? We've got to wait behind all
these people?" he groaned.

"I'm afraid so," sighed Mum.

"But we'll miss the plane! Why can't
we go to that desk?"

He pointed to the next one, where
no one was waiting.

"That's not our airline," said Dad.
"We're flying with Cheapy Jet."

Dirty Bertie

They joined the queue and waited as it shuffled forward at a snail's pace.

"Can I push the trolley?" begged Bertie.

"No," said Dad.

"But Suzy's had her turn!"

"Don't argue!" snapped Dad.

Bertie let go of the trolley. Dad had been in a bad mood since breakfast.

Dirty Bertie

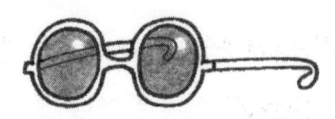

After half an hour they reached the desk and got their boarding passes. Next they queued at Passport Control. Then they joined the end of the snaking line at security. Finally, they had to wait an hour at the gate because their flight was delayed. Bertie couldn't believe catching a plane took so long. With buses you just got on!

At long last it was time to board. Bertie hurtled up the steps.

"Bags I sit by the window!" he cried, racing down the gangway. There were three seats to a row. Bertie plonked himself down by the window and took out his sweets.

"Who's sitting with Bertie?" asked Dad.

Dirty Bertie

"You can," said Mum, quickly. "I'll sit behind with Suzy."

Dad sank into his seat. Bertie was staring out of the window, sucking a fruity chew. At last, this was it – he was actually going to fly!

"Aren't you excited?" he asked, bouncing up and down.

"Not really," said Dad. "Fasten your seatbelt."

Dirty Bertie

Bertie wasn't listening. He reached up to a switch above him.

"What's this?"

CLICK! A light came on.

"A reading light," said Dad. "Leave it alone."

"And what does this one do?" asked Bertie, fiddling with a catch on the seat in front.

CLONK! A table flopped down, knocking his sweets out of his hand. Bertie scrambled on the floor to find them. Dad shut his eyes. Three hours on a plane with Bertie! He didn't know if his nerves could stand it.

None of the other passengers seemed to want the seat next to them. Eventually, a tall, elderly man sat down. He had big pink ears and a grumpy expression.

Bertie leaned over. "It's my first time on a plane," he said.

"Really," said Big Ears.

"Yes. Is it yours?"

"No," said Big Ears. He shook open his newspaper and hid behind it.

"Welcome aboard this Cheapy Jet Flight 647," said a voice over the tannoy. "Please listen carefully while we go through the safety procedures…"

Bertie leaned forward to watch as the flight attendants waved their arms.

"There are three emergency exits:
here, here and here…"

"What's an emergency exit?" Bertie
whispered.

"It's the way out in an emergency,"
said Dad.

"What sort of emergency?"

Dad sighed. "It doesn't matter."

"You mean like if one of the wings
drops off?" asked Bertie.

"Hopefully that won't happen," replied
Dad, loosening his collar.

Dirty Bertie

The voice went on. "You'll find a life jacket under your seat…"

"Have I got one?" Bertie asked.

"Yes," said Dad.

"Can I put it on now?"

"No!" groaned Dad. "It's only for … well, if we came down in the sea."

"In the sea? WOW!" said Bertie. "You mean like if we crash-land because the plane's on fire…"

"Bertie, *please!*" moaned Dad.

"I was only asking," said Bertie.

The plane shook as the engines rumbled into life. Dad gripped the arms of his seat.

"This is it. We're going!" cried Bertie.

Dad closed his eyes. He seemed to be praying. The plane bumped out towards the runway. It swung sharp left then

began to pick up speed. Dad shrank
back in his seat. Bertie had his nose
glued to the window, so he didn't miss
a thing.

"We're up!" he yelled. "Wahoo! Look,
you can see the airport. And the cars!
They're tiny, look!"

Dirty Bertie

Dad moaned. "I don't want to look!"

"Why not?" asked Bertie.

"Because I hate flying, okay? It makes me nervous."

Bertie frowned. How could anyone hate flying? It was brilliant – even better than going on a roller coaster.

CHAPTER 3

Bertie stared out of the window at the vast blue sky. They'd been flying for ages now. Dad was listening to music on his headphones. Bertie had eaten all his sweets. He was bored. A flight attendant came past pushing the drinks trolley. Her badge said "Tina".

Bertie nudged Dad.

Dirty Bertie

"Can I have some crisps?"

"What? No!"

"How about a Coke?"

"You're not having anything," said Dad. "Read your comic."

Bertie sighed. He had already read his comic *and* done his sticker book. It turned out they weren't even showing a film. No wonder the airline was called Cheapy Jet! He found a button on his armrest that he hadn't tried yet.

CLUNK!

His seat suddenly flipped backwards.

Dirty Bertie

"OWW!" wailed Suzy. "Mum!"

"Bertie!" sighed Mum.

"It wasn't my fault," said Bertie. "How was I to know it did that?"

"Just sit still and leave things alone," said Mum.

Bertie tilted his seat back up. He'd been sitting still for ages. His bottom ached. He poked Dad again.

"What now?" said Dad, removing his headphones.

"I need the toilet!" said Bertie.

Dad sighed. "It's at the front."

Bertie clambered past Dad and Big Ears and made his way down the aisle. He had to pass Tina, who was heading back with the drinks trolley. Bertie eyed the bags of crisps hungrily.

"Can I help you?" asked Tina.

"I need the toilet," said Bertie.

"It's occupied at the moment. You can wait outside," said Tina.

She disappeared behind a grey curtain with the trolley. Bertie stood tapping his feet. Whoever was in the toilet was taking ages! He wondered what happened when you flushed the loo on a plane. Did everything shoot out into the sky? Tina came out again and went down the aisle with the trolley.

Dirty Bertie

Bertie stared at the curtain. Maybe that was where the drinks and snacks were kept – the ones nobody wanted? It seemed a pity to waste them. No one was about, so he slipped through the curtain. He found himself looking at a wall of metal cases. Bertie tried to open one, but it wouldn't budge. Then he spotted something else – a panel of switches and buttons on the wall. At the top – just in reach – was a large red button.

Dirty Bertie

Bertie had been told a million times
not to touch things, especially things like
worms and snails. But buttons were
different. Bertie loved pressing them
because he wanted to know what they
did. Maybe this one fired the booster
rockets? Or set the plane to warp
speed? Bertie reached out a finger and
pressed…

WOOP! WOOP! WOOP! WOOP!

Yikes! A red light began to flash.

Bertie ducked back through the
curtain just as Tina came hurrying up
the gangway.

"I'm sorry, you'll have to return to
your seat," she said.

"But I still need the toilet," said Bertie.

"The seatbelt sign is on. Everyone
must take their seats," said Tina firmly.

Dirty Bertie

Bertie headed back, with the alarm ringing in his ears. People were looking round. This was not good. What if they found out it was him who set off the alarm? Maybe he'd be arrested. Or thrown out of the emergency exit!

CHAPTER 4

Bertie sank back in his seat.

"What's going on?" asked Dad.

"I don't know!" said Bertie. "I only went to the toilet."

Dad clutched at the arm of his seat.

"What's that alarm? Is something wrong?" he worried.

"It's probably just a mistake," said Bertie.

Dirty Bertie

"A fire alarm or something."

"*A FIRE ALARM?*" cried Dad.

"Did you say *fire*?" shouted Big Ears.

Bertie wished he'd never mentioned it.

"I didn't say there *was*…" he began.

But it was too late. The rumour was spreading from one row to the next.

"A fire? Where?"

"I don't know."

Dirty Bertie

"Someone said they smelled smoke!"

"It's one of the engines!"

"Good grief! Are we going to be all right?"

Dad had gone white. He was breathing heavily. Big Ears was arguing loudly with the man in front. A baby started wailing. Bertie sunk down in his seat. *Help!* he thought. *All I did was press one little button!*

Dirty Bertie

A voice on the tannoy rang out. "If I can have your attention! Everyone *please* stay in their seats. There is no reason to panic."

Flight attendants hurried to and fro, trying to calm everyone down.

Tina came past.

"What's that alarm?" Big Ears demanded.

"Nothing to worry about, sir," said Tina.

"Are we on fire?"

"No, of course not," said Tina.

Dirty Bertie

WOOP! WOOP! WOO—

The alarm suddenly stopped. Silence fell. It was broken by a new voice over the tannoy.

"Captain Rogers here. Awfully sorry about that. It seems someone set off an alarm by mistake. Anyway, no harm done. Please remain seated while the cabin crew come round and serve refreshments."

Everyone breathed a huge sigh of relief. Big Ears went back to his paper, muttering to himself. Dad slumped back in his seat, exhausted. Bertie puffed out his cheeks.

Tina appeared again, pushing the drinks trolley.

"Any drinks? Tea, coffee, juice?" she asked.

"Tea," said Big Ears. "And maybe you

can tell me exactly how this alarm went off?"

"We don't know, sir," said Tina. "It could have been a passenger."

"Where was it?"

Tina pointed. "In the serving area, past the toilet."

Dad frowned. A worrying thought crossed his mind. Where was Bertie when the alarm went off? He turned to him.

Dirty Bertie

"*Did you have anything to do with this?*"

"M-me?" gulped Bertie.

"Yes, you. Did you set off the alarm?"

"No!" said Bertie. "I never touched it!"

"Touched what?" said Dad.

"You know … the thing … the red button."

Dad narrowed his eyes. "How do you know it's a red button?" he said.

"Um…" said Bertie.

Nobody spoke much to Bertie for the rest of the flight. Dad kept his headphones on. Mum had her nose in her book. Now and again, other passengers turned round to glare in Bertie's direction.

Dirty Bertie

At last, the plane came in to land. Dad grabbed their bags and they hurried off.

At the bottom of the steps a young man was waiting. He handed them a card.

"Would you like to fill in our Cheapy Jet survey?" he asked. "You could win a free flight for all the family."

"A free flight?" said Dad.

"Fantastic!" cried Bertie.

Mum and Dad looked down at him.

"No, thanks," said Dad, handing back the card. "We are *never* going on a plane again!"

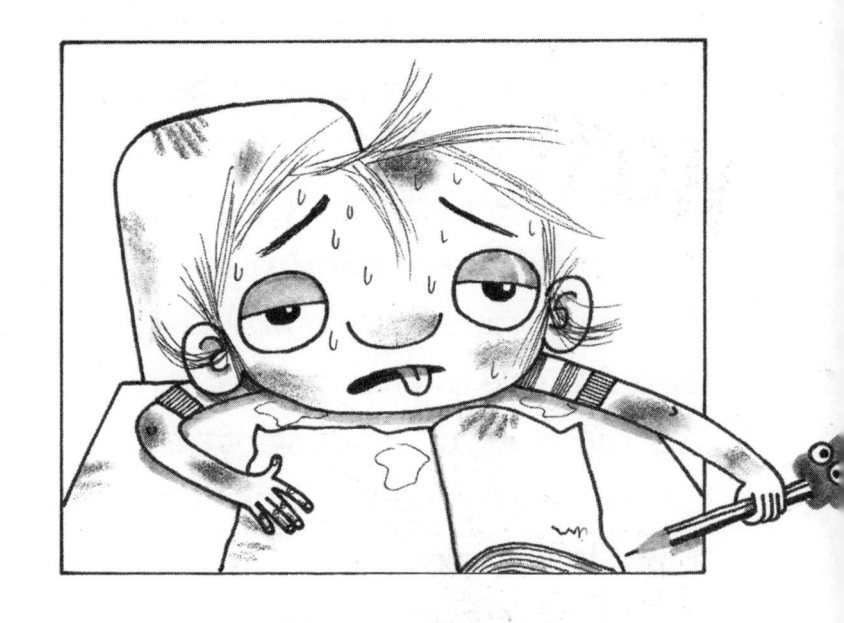

CHAPTER 1

It was hot. Scorching hot. Sitting at the back of the class, Bertie felt he was going to melt. It was ages till afternoon break. His head flopped on to his desk. He was certain it must be 1000 degrees. There ought to be a law against going to school in this heat.

It was all right for teachers, he thought

Dirty Bertie

bitterly. Miss Boot had a fan on her desk to keep her cool. The rest of them had to roast. Eugene's cheeks had gone bright pink. Darren's hair was sticking up like a paintbrush. Only Know-All Nick looked as pale and neat as ever.

Bertie moaned. "I'm dying of thirst!"

"Me, too," said Darren. "Ask Miss Boot if we can get a drink."

"You ask her," replied Bertie.

Darren raised his hand.

"Miss, please may I go to the toilet?"

"Certainly not. Wait till break time,"
snapped Miss Boot.

Darren squirmed in his seat.

"Pleeeeease! I've been holding on
since lunchtime!"

Miss Boot rolled her eyes.

"Oh, very well."

Darren got up, giving Bertie a wink as
he left the class. There was a drinking
fountain by the boys' toilets. Bertie
watched him go and stuck up his hand.

"Miss…"

"No, you can't," snapped Miss Boot.

"But Miss, I…"

"No means NO!" thundered Miss
Boot.

Bertie's shoulders slumped. It was so
unfair! How come Darren got to go and

he didn't? He glanced up at the clock.
He'd never last till break. He was actually
dying of thirst. Soon he'd be nothing but
clothes in a puddle of sweat.

DING-A-DING! DING-A-DING!

Bertie sat up. He knew that sound.
It was Mr Frosty's
ice-cream van! The
van tootled down
the road, playing
its merry tune, and
parked near the
school gates. Bertie
stared out of the window.
What he would give now for a juicy
Cola-Cooler lolly! Or an extra-large
cone with soft ice cream…

"BERTIE!"

Miss Boot was standing over him.

Dirty Bertie

"Yes, Miss?"

"Get on with your work. You haven't written two words."

Bertie sighed. It was cruelty. He *needed* an ice cream. Besides, ice cream was good for you. It contained healthy stuff like um … cream. If Miss Boot wasn't such a meanie, she would go and buy him one.

CHAPTER 2

At break time Bertie and his friends stood staring out through the fence. They watched the nursery children come out and get ice creams.

This is torture, thought Bertie. The van was parked ten metres up the road, but it might as well have been a million miles. School was just like prison.

Dirty Bertie

The gates were locked and the teachers were on patrol at all times.

"There *must* be a way," said Bertie.

"Face it," said Eugene. "It's impossible."

Darren nodded. "Forget it."

Bertie flopped against the fence. All he wanted was one teeny-weeny ice cream (with a chocolate flake). Was that too much to ask? If he closed his eyes, he could almost taste it. Smooth, silky ice cream slipping down his throat.

He opened his eyes and stared at the fence. There had to be a way out somewhere… Hang on, what was that? A little further along, the wire fence was bent back. It left a tiny gap underneath, big enough for a cat or a small person to crawl through. They could escape! There was just one problem – Miss Boot was on playground duty. If she spotted them, she'd swoop down like a fire-breathing dragon.

Bertie racked his brains. They needed some way to distract her. But what? Eugene tap-dancing? Know-All Nick yelling that his pants were on fire? What would get Miss Boot's *full* attention? Bertie smiled. He knew just the thing.

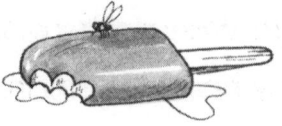

Miss Boot sat on a bench in the shade, fanning herself with her sun hat. Darren wandered over.

"Miss," he said. "What do rats look like?"

Miss Boot frowned. "Rats?" she said. "They're like mice, only bigger and dirtier. Why?"

"Oh, nothing. It's just I thought I saw one," said Darren.

Miss Boot turned pale. *Rats? In the school?* If there was one thing she hated it was rats. Filthy, horrible vermin!

"Where?" she said.

"Over there," said Darren, pointing to the rubbish bins.

Miss Boot followed him over. She was certain Darren had imagined it. All the same, she didn't want to get too close, just in case. If there was a rat, it might run over her foot – or even up her leg. She shuddered at the thought.

Dirty Bertie

"Where was it?" she demanded.

"Just there, Miss, by the bin," said Darren. "A great big rat with blood-red eyes and pointy teeth."

Miss Boot went a bit closer. She bent down to look.

THUMP!

Suddenly, one of the bins jumped.

Dirty Bertie

"ARRRRRGHH!" screamed Miss Boot, leaping back. If that was a rat, it was a monster. A king rat!

"I'll er … I'll fetch Mr Grouch," she gulped. "Rats are his job, really. Keep away from there, Darren."

She hurried off to find the caretaker.

As soon as she was gone, Eugene popped up from behind the bin.

"Did it work?" he asked.

"Like a dream," said Darren. He hurried over to Bertie by the fence.

"All clear?" said Bertie.

"Yes, but you'd better be quick," said Darren, holding up the fence.

Dirty Bertie

They didn't have long. Miss Boot
would be back any minute with Mr
Grouch. Bertie looked around. No one
was watching. He got down and
squeezed through the small hole. Now
to grab the ice creams and make it back
before anyone saw him.

CHAPTER 3

Bertie waited, hopping from foot to foot. There were two other people in the queue and they were taking ages. At any moment he expected to hear Miss Boot screeching his name. At last he reached the front.

"Three large cones, please," he said. "With sprinkles and a chocolate flake."

Dirty Bertie

He watched the smooth, soft ice cream ooze from the nozzle.

"Three pounds," said the ice-cream man.

Bertie handed over the money they'd scraped together and grabbed the cones. He'd been dreaming of this moment all day. He lifted one of the ice creams to his mouth…

DRRRRING!

Bertie looked up. No way! Surely that couldn't be the bell already?

But the playground was starting to empty. His class were lining up under the stern eye of Miss Boot. Bertie quickly ducked out of sight behind a tree.

Dirty Bertie

Darren stood in line with Eugene. He glanced back towards the fence. There was no sign of Bertie. What was he playing at? A hand tapped him on the shoulder. He turned round to see Know-All Nick's smug face.

"Where's Bertie?" Nick asked.

"How should I know?" shrugged Darren. "He's here somewhere."

Nick looked around. "Really? I don't see him. Shall I tell Miss Boot?"

"Mind your own business," said Darren.

"No talking!" shouted Miss Boot. They trooped inside.

Bertie came out from behind the tree and stared at the empty playground.

Help! Now what? He couldn't crawl under the fence without Darren to hold it up. And anyway, he had his hands full of ice creams. This was terrible! He'd escaped, but now he couldn't get back in!

Dirty Bertie

Ice cream dripped down his fingers.
How could he give Darren and Eugene
their cornets now? But if he hung on to
them, they'd only melt! It seemed a pity
to let them go to waste. Bertie licked his
own ice cream, then the other two.

All his class would be sitting down
now. And Miss Boot would be sure
to notice his empty chair. Sooner or
later she'd worm the truth out of
Darren and Eugene. Then a search
party would be sent out with sniffer
dogs. If they found him, he was in BIG
trouble. Miss Boot would move him
away from his friends. He'd have to sit
at the front – probably next to a GIRL!
Bertie felt ill at the thought. Somehow
he had to get back into school.

As he stood there, a lorry drew up

and the driver jumped out.

"S'cuse me, son, is this Pudsley Junior?" he asked.

Bertie nodded.

"Thanks," said the driver. He looked at Bertie and frowned. "Shouldn't you be in school?"

"Er no," said Bertie. "I'm um … off sick."

"Right. So you're buying ice creams?"

"Oh no, they're not mine, I'm just looking after them," explained Bertie.

"Course you are," smiled the driver. He went back to the lorry, laughing to himself. Another man got out, and together they unloaded two large boxes from the back of the lorry. Bertie watched, licking his three cones.

The driver went to the gates and
spoke into the intercom. A moment later,
the gates began to open and the men
carried one of the boxes inside. *This is it*,
thought Bertie, *my chance to get in!* But
wait – what about Mrs Duff, the school
secretary? No one got past her eagle
eyes. There had to be another way.
Bertie looked at the remaining cardboard

Dirty Bertie

box sitting beside the lorry. Quickly, he opened it up. Inside were some flat bits of wood and a bag of screws. Maybe there was just enough room? Clutching his ice cream cones, Bertie climbed into the box.

CHAPTER 4

A few minutes later, the two men returned.

"This one as well? What's in them?" said the driver's mate.

"How should I know? Just pick it up."

Bertie heard a lot of grunting and felt the box lift off the ground.

"It weighs a ton! They got a dead

body in here?"

Inside the box, Bertie hardly dared to breathe. All he had to do was wait till the box was set down. Then he could slip out quietly and sneak back to his class. With a bit of luck, Miss Boot hadn't even noticed he was missing. He licked one of the cones – no point in saving them now…

Back in class, Darren and Eugene were starting to worry.

"Where is he?" hissed Eugene.

"Search me," said Darren. "Where are our ice creams?"

"Maybe he can't get back under the fence," worried Eugene. He looked round and caught Know-All Nick's eye.

Dirty Bertie

Trust that nosy creep to be snooping around, thought Eugene. *How much does he know? Did he see Bertie escape? Uh-oh, he's putting his hand up.*

"Miss Boot," said Nick. "Where's Bertie?"

Miss Boot looked up. "Bertie?" She stared at the empty chair where Bertie normally sat.

"Where *is* Bertie?" she demanded.

"I don't know," said Nick slyly. "I haven't seen him since break. Maybe he's run away!"

Miss Boot frowned. "Darren? Do you know?"

Darren's mind was a blank. "Oh he's er … he's…"

"…He's gone to wash his hands," said Eugene, quickly.

"Why?" said Miss Boot.

"They were dirty," said Eugene.

Miss Boot narrowed her eyes. Bertie's hands were always dirty, but he'd never felt the need to wash them before. Besides, it was ten minutes since break. Where had the dratted boy got to this time? Knowing Bertie, he was somewhere he shouldn't be.

"Give him one minute, then go and fetch him," she ordered.

Just then there was a knock at the door.

Two men in blue overalls shuffled in, carrying a large box.

"Delivery," panted one of them. "Where do you want it?"

"Put it over there," said Miss Boot.

Dirty Bertie

She had been waiting for the new TV cabinet for weeks. But she could deal with that later, once she'd found Bertie.

Inside the box, Bertie was getting cramp. His knees were squashed in his face. Maybe it was safe to get out now? He peeped through a tiny hole in the box. He could see a thick pair of woollen tights. Yikes! He knew those tree-trunk legs – they were Miss Boot's! He was back in his own classroom.

There was nothing for it but to sit tight and wait till everyone went home. At least he still had one cone left.

CRUNCH!

Know-All Nick looked up. What was that noise? It had come from the box. Should he tell Miss Boot? He shot up his hand.

Dirty Bertie

"Miss!"

"Not now, Nicholas," sighed Miss Boot.

"But Miss, I think there's something in the box," said Nick.

"Yes, it's a TV cabinet," said Miss Boot.

"But I heard it, Miss, it made a noise!"

Miss Boot frowned. First it was rats by the bins, now strange noises – there was something funny going on. She approached the cardboard box. Eugene and Darren looked at each other. Surely it couldn't be...?

Miss Boot ripped opened the flaps. She gasped.

A face rose slowly from the box. Bertie had ice cream round his mouth. Large blobs had dripped all down his shirt.

"The greedy pig!" gasped Darren. "He ate them all!"

"BERTIE!" boomed Miss Boot. "What *are* you doing in there?"

"Um … well…" said Bertie.

Miss Boot pulled him out by the arm. "Wait, what is that on your face?" she said.

Dirty Bertie

"Have you been eating *ice cream*?"

Bertie swallowed. He brought out a messy blob from his pocket.

"Chocolate flake?" he said.